Original Korean text by Mi-ok Lee
Illustrations by Edmée Cannard
Korean edition © Yeowon Media Co., Ltd.

This English edition published by big & SMALL in 2015
by arrangement with Yeowon Media Co., Ltd.
English text edited by Joy Cowley
English edition © big & SMALL 2015

All photo images used are in the public domain, except:
page 43 "Cossi fan tutti" © jjsala - Houston, USA (Opera in the Heights) (CC BY 2.0)

ISBN: 978-1-925233-76-6

Printed in Korea

Mozart's
# The Magic Flute

Retold by Mi-ok Lee
Illustrated by Edmée Cannard
Edited by Joy Cowley

big & SMALL

The Queen of the Night gives Tamino a magic flute
made from a one-thousand-year-old oak tree.
The flute is said to bring love and good fortune to people.
Will it help Prince Tamino in his quest for love?

**Prince Tamino**

He falls in love with a portrait of Princess Pamina,

and sets out on an adventure to find love.

## Princess Pamina

She is the daughter of the Queen of the Night.

## The Queen of the Night

She controls darkness and represents evil.

## Papageno

He is a bird-catcher dressed in feathers. He wants to meet a wonderful lady.

## Papagena

She appears as an old woman but changes into a young lady dressed in feathers.

## Monostatos

He is the captain of Sarastro's guards and loves Princess Pamina.

## Sarastro

He is high priest of the sun god and represents good. He wears a necklace with a seven-layer gold medallion.

Prince Tamino was out hunting in the forest
when he got lost.
A large snake slithered towards him.
No matter how fast he ran, the snake followed.
When Prince Tamino tripped on a rock,
the snake drew close and opened its mouth wide.
Prince Tamino fainted.

As the snake was about to swallow the prince,
it suddenly fell to the ground.
Three ladies of the Queen of the Night
had used their magic powers to kill it.
The ladies looked at Prince Tamino.
"He is such a handsome young man!" they said.
"Let's hurry and tell the queen about him!"
They ran off to find the Queen of the Night.

Prince Tamino woke up. "Where am I?"
He looked around and saw the dead snake
and Papageno dressed in rainbow feathers.
Papageno made bird noises as he approached.

♪ "I am the bird-catcher,
   and I am always happy, heidi heh hey!
   Wherever I go in the world, everyone knows
   I am the happy bird-catcher."

"That's a great song," said Prince Tamino.
"Thank you very much for rescuing me."

Papageno was bewildered, but then played along.
"It was tough to kill that huge snake!" said Papageno.

The ladies of the Queen of the Night returned
and heard Papageno's boastful lie.
"Papageno! *We* killed that giant snake!"
As a punishment, they put a lock on his mouth.
Then they handed a portrait to Prince Tamino.
"This is our queen's daughter, Princess Pamina."

As soon as Prince Tamino looked at the picture,
he fell in love with the princess.
He kissed the portrait, his heart beating fast.

♪ *"She is so beautiful it drives me crazy.*
*No one has seen such an angel before!*
*Staring at this divine face,*
*my heart is filled with joy."*

The three ladies led Tamino and Papageno
to the palace of the Queen of the Night.

*Boom! Boom!* The night was split by thunder
around the palace of the Queen of the Night.
The queen summoned Prince Tamino.
"Sarastro has captured my daughter, Pamina!
Rescue her and she will be yours forever!"

Prince Tamino nodded, and the queen disappeared.
The ladies came forward with a magic flute.
As they gave it to the prince, they told him,
"This magic flute brings love and fortune to people.
When you're in trouble, blow on it
and you will be helped."

The ladies unlocked Papageno's mouth
and gave him a magic bell. They told him,
"You will get a wife if you follow the prince."

The ladies then sent three boys to ride in a balloon
to guide Prince Tamino and Papageno to Sarastro's castle.

Before they reached the castle,
Prince Tamino and Papageno got separated.
Papageno arrived at the castle first.

Papageno entered just as Monostatos, the captain
of Sarastro's guards was trying to kiss the princess.

"Help me!" cried Princess Pamina.

When Papageno and Monostatos caught sight of each other,
they both shrieked, "Ah! It's a beast!"
They ran away in fright.

However, Papageno returned to the princess and told her
that Prince Tamino was coming to rescue her.
This made the princess's heart beat faster.

The three boys in the balloon
led Prince Tamino to Sarastro's temple,
which stood beside his castle.

When the prince knocked on the door,
a priest appeared and asked why he had come.

"I am here to rescue Princess Pamina
from the evil Sarastro," said the prince.

"No, it's the other way around," said the priest.
"Sarastro has saved Princess Pamina
from the wicked Queen of the Night.
You should know that there are two worlds here,
the dark world ruled by the Queen of the Night
and the world of goodness ruled by Sarastro."

This confused Prince Tamino,
so he played a tune on his magic flute.
Animals and birds began to dance and sing,
and from somewhere in the nearby castle
came the sound of Papageno's bell.

17

Papageno and Princess Pamina followed
the sounds of the flute to the temple.
Monostatos also heard the flute
and his servants caught Papageno and the princess.
But as they tried to grab Princess Pamina,
Papageno rang the magic bell
and Monostatos and his servants danced away.

At that moment, a trumpet sounded
to announce the arrival of Sarastro.
"Please forgive me for trying to leave,"
the princess said to Sarastro.

"I only kept you here to protect you
from the Queen of the Night," he replied.
"However, I will not stop you now,
for you are about to find true love."

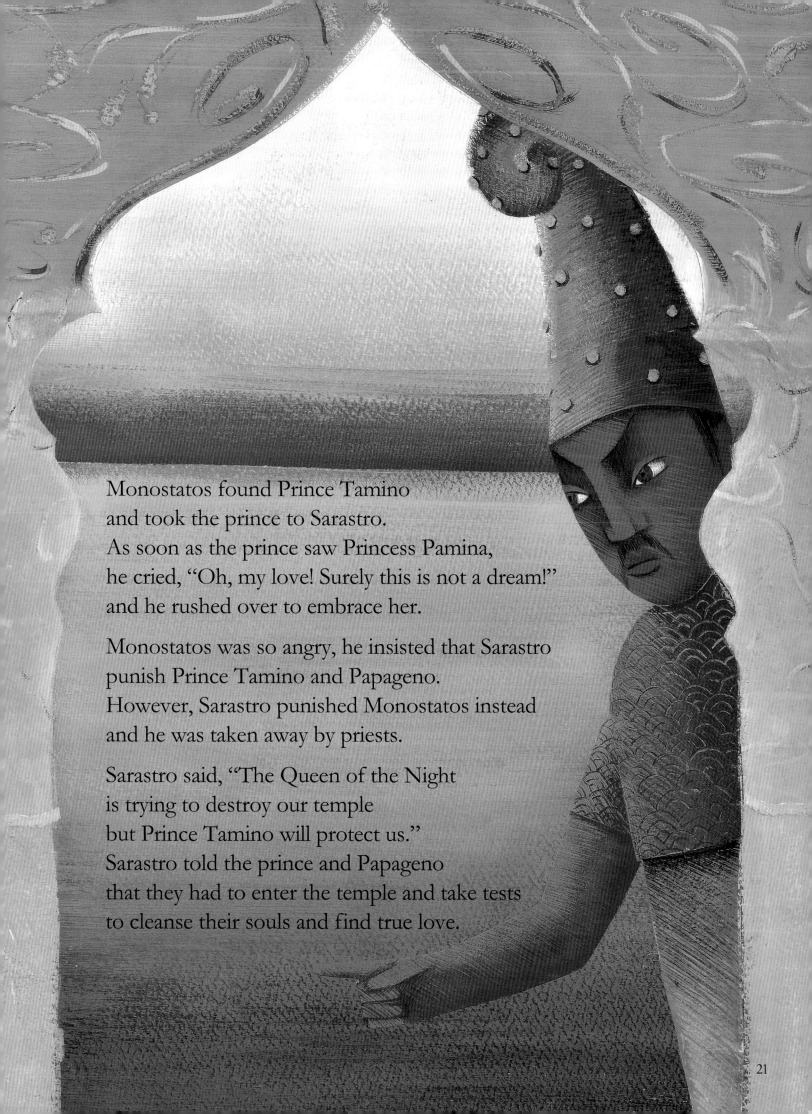

Monostatos found Prince Tamino
and took the prince to Sarastro.
As soon as the prince saw Princess Pamina,
he cried, "Oh, my love! Surely this is not a dream!"
and he rushed over to embrace her.

Monostatos was so angry, he insisted that Sarastro
punish Prince Tamino and Papageno.
However, Sarastro punished Monostatos instead
and he was taken away by priests.

Sarastro said, "The Queen of the Night
is trying to destroy our temple
but Prince Tamino will protect us."
Sarastro told the prince and Papageno
that they had to enter the temple and take tests
to cleanse their souls and find true love.

Late at night, Prince Tamino and Papageno
went into the temple. It was pitch black.
They could not even see each other.
A priest's voice asked, "What brings you here?"

The prince replied, "We come out of love and friendship.
I will risk my life for love."

To test their determination, the priest made
the prince and Papageno take a vow of silence.
Then maidservants appeared and tempted them
to speak with their beautiful, melodic voices.

But Prince Tamino and Papageno
refused to speak, and the women left.

Meanwhile, Princess Pamina was resting
in the garden when Monostatos entered.
Suddenly, there were sounds of thunder
and the Queen of the Night appeared.
Monostatos hid behind a tree.

The Queen of the Night said to the princess,
"My daughter, before your father died,
he gave Sarastro a gold sun necklace
that has great magical powers.
Since then, my powers have become weak.
Your father hoped Sarastro would protect you
but Sarastro is trying to destroy me.
Take this dagger and kill him!"

♪ *"The vengeance of hell boils in my heart.*
   *Death and despair blaze around me!"*

After she gave her daughter the dagger,
the Queen of the Night disappeared into the earth.

Monostatos came out from behind the tree,
and took the dagger from the princess.
"Aha! I will tell Sarastro about this plot.
Unless you say you love me, and then I will keep it secret."

But Sarastro appeared and chased Monostratos away.

Princess Pamina pleaded with Sarastro,
"Please, do not take revenge on my mother."

Sarastro replied:

♪ "There is no such thing as revenge in this divine temple,
because we forgive even our enemies."

27

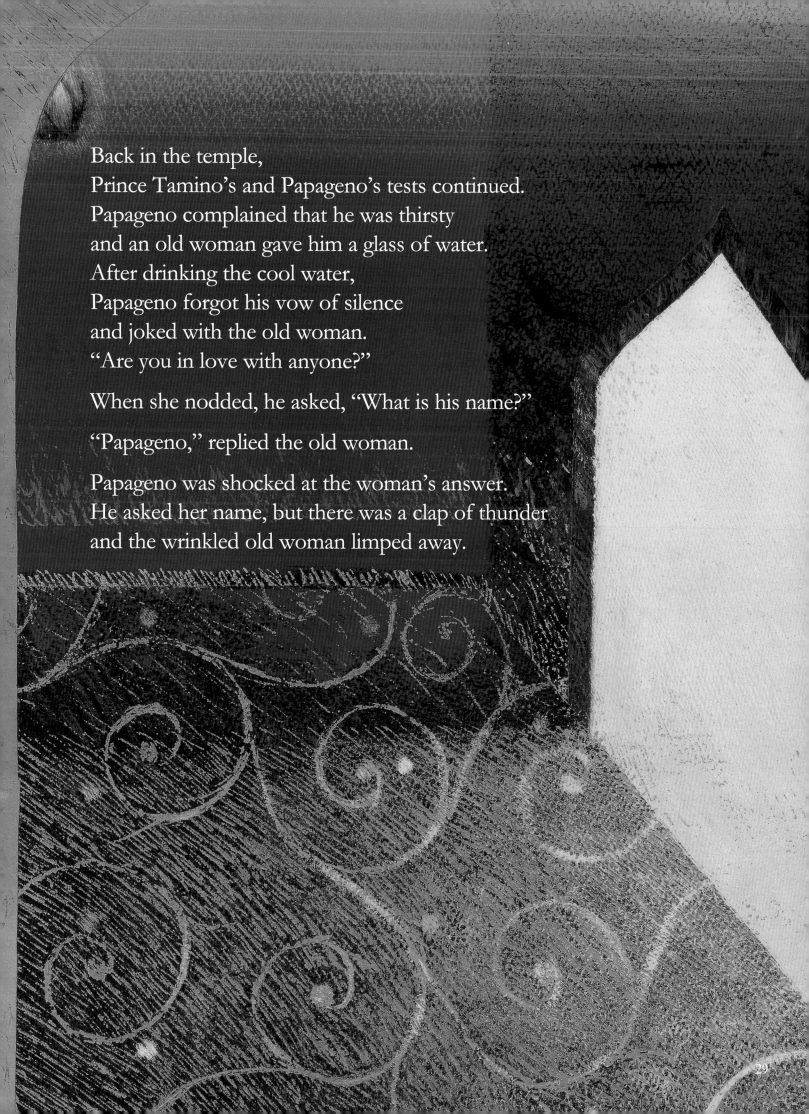

Back in the temple,
Prince Tamino's and Papageno's tests continued.
Papageno complained that he was thirsty
and an old woman gave him a glass of water.
After drinking the cool water,
Papageno forgot his vow of silence
and joked with the old woman.
"Are you in love with anyone?"

When she nodded, he asked, "What is his name?"

"Papageno," replied the old woman.

Papageno was shocked at the woman's answer.
He asked her name, but there was a clap of thunder
and the wrinkled old woman limped away.

The boys on the balloon came with food and words
of encouragement for the prince and Papageno.
Papageno enjoyed the food but Prince Tamino
was too busy thinking about the princess,
so he kept playing the magic flute.
Princess Pamina heard the flute and came,
but Prince Tamino couldn't talk to her.

"Don't you love me any more?" she asked.

Instead of answering, he waved his hand,
indicating she should go back.

Princess Pamina could not hide
her grief. She sang,

♪ "Ah, now everything is gone.
Forever gone, all my happiness.
Forever gone, love's happiness!"

Princess Pamina ran away crying,
but the three boys told her that Prince Tamino
had not changed and they would meet again.

The high priest Sarastro appeared
and congratulated the prince on passing the test of silence.
Leaving Papageno in the room,
he took Prince Tamino to meet Princess Pamina.

The prince and the princess embraced.
"Let us overcome fire and water,
with the power of our love," they agreed.
Princess Pamina told the prince to play the magic flute
as they passed through chambers of fire and water.
"The magic flute will protect us," she said.

When a ball of fire fell on Prince Tamino,
he played the flute and the fire flickered and went out.
When he ran into a crashing pillar of water,
he played his flute and the water became calm.

Prince Tamino and Princess Pamina
successfully survived fire and water.

Meanwhile, Papageno could not leave the room,
as he had broken the vow of silence.
The old woman reappeared and told him that
if he swore his love for her, he would get a wife.
If he did not, he would be trapped in the room forever.

Papageno thought it better to have an old wife
than to be trapped, so he swore his love.
At once, the old woman changed into a young lady
called Papagena, who wore clothes of beautiful feathers.
But before Papageno could show his joy,
Papagena vanished, and he was very upset.

The three boys appeared and said,
"Ring the magic bell. That will get her back."
Papageno shook the bell and Papagena appeared.
The happy couple embraced and sang:

♪ "Pa, Pa, Pa, Papageno..."
"Pa, Pa, Pa, Papagena..."

The Queen of the Night and her three ladies
came with Monostatos to the temple.
They plotted to destroy the temple.
When Monostatos opened the temple door,
a blinding light poured out, and the queen
could not get away from its powerful strength.
They fell down into deep darkness
and a new world of bright sunlight opened.
Sarastro gave Prince Tamino the sun necklace.
"The shining sun has overcome the darkness!"

A joyful wedding was held
for Prince Tamino and Princess Pamina.

# 9: Let's Learn About **The Magic Flute**

## 🎵 Wolfgang Amadeus Mozart

**Born:** 27 January 1756

**Died:** 5 December 1791

**Place of birth:** Salzburg, Austria

**Biography:** An Austrian composer, pianist, violinist, violist and conductor, Mozart is regarded as the most talented musician in history. Born into a musical family, Mozart showed talent from an early age. He composed his first piece of music when he was five, a symphony at eight, and his first opera at eleven. By his early twenties, he was recognised as one of Europe's greatest musicians and composers.

His symphonies and operas became famous. However, he was not good at organising his finances and struggled with poverty throughout his life. He finished the opera *The Magic Flute* two months before he died at the age of thirty-five. Mozart composed over 600 works in his short life.

**Major works:**

1785 *Piano Concerto No. 20 in D minor*

1786 *The Marriage of Figaro*

1787 *Don Giovani*

1788 *Symphony No. 40*

1791 *The Magic Flute*

Mozart, his sister and his father performing.

The house in Salzburg where Mozart was born.

## 🏴 The Story of **The Magic Flute**

Mozart's opera was inspired by a short story published in Germany in 1786 called *Lulu*, or *The Magic Flute*. Mozart's *The Magic Flute* is the story of Prince Tamino, who loves the beautiful Princess Pamina, and the struggle between the Queen of the Night and Sarastro, the high priest of the sun god. The opera represents the fight between light and darkness, good and evil. Featuring lovely melodies and speech that is both spoken and sung, this opera is considered one of Mozart's greatest masterpieces. It is the only opera Mozart composed in German, so it is often performed in Germany. The German title is *Die Zauberflöte*.

Papageno the bird-catcher.

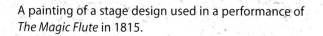

A painting of a stage design used in a performance of *The Magic Flute* in 1815.

# ♫ Let's Find Out About the Music

*The Magic Flute* is composed in the style of Singspiel, a type of German opera that includes both spoken and sung speech, and funny and romantic plots. Let's look at the arias* of brave Prince Tamino, beautiful Princess Pamina, carefree Papageno, and the evil Queen of the Night.

\* An aria is a long song sung by one person.

## I Am the Bird-catcher
### Papageno

This is the aria in which the bird-catcher Papageno introduces himself. It reveals his cheerful and outgoing character, which provides a lot of the comedy in *The Magic Flute*.

*"I am the bird-catcher,*
*and I am always happy, heidi heh hey!*
*Wherever I go in the world, everyone knows*
*I am the happy bird-catcher."*

## This Image Is Enchantingly Lovely
### Prince Tamino

Prince Tamino sings this aria when he falls in love with Princess Pamina as he sees the princess's portrait. It is about the strength of love at first sight.

*"She is so beautiful it drives me crazy.*
*No one has seen such an angel before!*
*Staring at this divine face,*
*my heart is filled with joy."*

## Hell's Vengeance Boils in My Heart
### The Queen of the Night

The Queen of the Night sings this famous aria to Princess Pamina as she hopes for revenge. The singer must hit a very high note over and over again, so it is a very difficult song.

*"The vengeance of hell boils in my heart.*
*Death and despair blaze around me!"*

## Within These Hallowed Halls
### Sarastro

When Princess Pamina begs Sarastro to forgive her mother, Sarastro sings this aria declaring that revenge will not be taken.

*"Within these hallowed halls,*
*one knows not revenge.*
*And should a person have fallen,*
*love will guide him to duty."*

## Ah, Everything Has Disappeared
### Princess Pamina

This is the aria that Princess Pamina sings when she is upset, believing Tamino no longer loves her. The princess doesn't know that Tamino is silent because he is being tested.

*"Ah, now everything is gone.*
*Forever gone, all my happiness.*
*Forever gone love's happiness!"*

# ♪ Let's Discover Mozart's Other Operas

Mozart took opera to a new level by using ordinary people as the main characters instead of great heroes or lords and ladies. This was popular with audiences, as people could relate to the characters better. His skill at combining the sounds of human voices and musical instruments allowed him to create some of the most memorable operas.

##  Don Giovanni

**Date:** 1787

**Background:** *Don Giovanni* was inspired by the legend of Don Juan, a character famous for not caring about right and wrong. Mozart's opera is probably the best-known appearance of this character.

**The story:** Don Giovanni kills the father of a woman he likes. But he doesn't regret this, and Don Giovanni keeps behaving badly. One night, he has dinner with the ghost of the man he killed. The ghost gives Don Giovanni one last chance to say he's sorry. But Don Giovanni refuses and so he dies and is carried away to hell.

A painting of a scene from *Don Giovanni*.

**Overview:** *Don Giovanni* has both funny and tragic elements and the main character is engaging and entertaining.

Stage design for a 1949 performance of *Don Giovanni*

# Cosi Fan Tutte

**Date:** 1790

**Background:** "Cosi fan tutte" means "women are like that" in Italian. Mozart wrote the music and the lyrics (the words) were written by an Italian man called Lorenzo Da Ponte.

**The story:** After making a bet, two army officers test the women they plan to marry by disguising themselves as other men and pretending to like them. Unaware of the trick, the women find themselves in all sorts of trouble. In the end, the trick is revealed, the women are relieved and everyone lives happily ever after.

**Overview:** *Cosi Fan Tutte* is much loved for its light-hearted nature. There is a cheerful and funny selection of beautiful songs.

A scene from a production of *Cosi Fan Tutte*.

# The Marriage of Figaro

**Date:** 1786

**Background:** This opera is based on a popular play at the time, which had the same title.

**The story:** All the action takes place on the wedding day of Figaro and his sweetheart Susanna. When an old debt Figaro owes is discovered, the wedding is threatened. With a bit of luck and some help from unlikely places, Figaro succeeds and is able to marry Susanna.

**Overview:** This is a love story with lots of twists and turns. Its orchestral prelude (beginning) is so famous that it is often played separately. Many of the arias in this opera are also very popular.

A painting of a scene from *The Marriage of Figaro*.